CONTENTS

Bored!

On Sunday morning, I put on my slippers and shuffle into the kitchen. A note on the table reads: *Breakfast outside!*

I roll my eyes. Since moving here a month ago for my dad's job, my parents have eaten outside almost daily. They say they want to "be closer to nature".

Personally, I don't see what's so great about nature. Our old city had more noise than nature. I like it better that way.

Still, I know they'll be upset if I don't join them. Reluctantly, I head outside to join them.

"Morning, sleepyhead!" Mum chirps from the table.

Dad draws an exaggerated breath. "Can't you just taste the fresh air?"

I take a seat and pour some cereal and milk into my bowl. "All I can taste is cereal," I say between bites. "I had that in our old house."

Dad sighs. "Is hating everything part of your twelve-year-old rule book?"

I scowl. "It's not about my age. I just haven't found anything to like yet."

There is *nothing to like*, I think privately. *Everything good is back in our old city – my home, my friends and my dance school.*

At that moment, a familiar ringtone chimes. It belongs to Maya, my best friend. Dad shoots me his no-phones-at-the-table look.

"Sorry," I mumble, quickly silencing my phone.

My parents exchange glances. The last time I caught them doing that, they'd announced we were moving. *Not* a good sign.

Mum clears her throat. "I was going to surprise you, but this seems like a good time to tell you."

My parents are smiling. Maybe this is a good surprise after all.

"Tell me what?" I ask.

"I've found a dance studio nearby," Mum continues. "It has a team you can audition for. Students focus on different types of dance – jazz, ballet, hip-hop and tap – just like at your old studio."

I want to sulk, but I can't. "Thank you!" I exclaim. I've practised my old ballet routine several times since we moved, but dancing with a team is way more fun than practising solo.

Maybe there's hope for this town yet.

CHAPTER 2

A NEW STUDIO

The following week, I sit in my mum's car and stare out of the window at a building that looks like a one-room schoolhouse from old films. From the outside, Ms Marianne's Academy of Dance is not exactly impressive.

"What's wrong?" Mum asks. "This morning, you were so excited about your audition."

I slump in my seat. "How do they even fit studios in there?"

Mum sighs. "I know your old dance studio looked bigger and more impressive, but looks can be deceiving."

"I suppose."

She turns off the car. "Do you want me to go in with you?"

I do, but I don't want to walk inside with my *mummy* and have the other dancers laugh at me. "I'll be OK."

Mum hugs me. "Just keep an open mind."

How bad could it be if it has a dance team? I think as I grab my bag and jog to the door.

My mouth drops open when I walk in. Studios line the corridors. Through the open doorways, I can see floor-to-ceiling mirrors and barres. Sunbeams dance across the shiny, hardwood floors. I feel silly for judging the place so harshly minutes before.

Taking a deep breath, I head for the first small room along the corridor. The word *OFFICE* is written in big, bold letters on the door. Inside, a woman with curly blonde hair and a friendly smile sits at the desk.

"Um, I'm Jada Grant," I say. "I'm here to audition."

The woman scans a list next to her computer. "Yes, here you are. I'm Ms Jenkins." She steps out from behind her desk. "You'll love it here."

Her kind voice helps me relax. "I hope so."

She laughs. "My daughter Grace was new last year, so I understand what it's like. I'll show you the changing rooms."

We head down the corridor to a room with brightly painted lockers. I put away my bag, then follow Ms Jenkins back to the office.

"Auditions don't start for half an hour," says Ms Jenkins, "but you can warm up if you'd like. The third studio on the left is free. The other girls should be arriving soon."

I bite my lip, feeling nervous. *What if they're all better dancers than I am?* I worry. *What if they don't want anyone new on the team?*

I try to ignore the negative thoughts and walk to the studio. I run a hand across the smooth, wooden barre and close my eyes. Here, it doesn't matter whether I'm in the city or not. When I dance, I focus on only one thing – ballet.

I begin with *pliés*, one of the first moves I'd learned when I started dancing seven years before. Turning out my toes, I bend my knees, sinking into the *plié*, then rise back up. My arms curve in front of my stomach so my fingertips almost touch, then overhead to fifth position.

As I go through my warm-up, my former dance teacher's voice plays in my head: "Show them some *attitude!*"

I smile. The pun always made me laugh, but it worked – I never forgot that position.

I move into *attitude* now, raising one leg high behind my body and bending it at a ninety-degree angle.

Thinking about my former teacher makes me think of Maya and another teammate, Natalie. *What are they doing right now? Probably dancing too*, I realize. *With everyone else from my team. Correction – my* former *team.*

I try to forget everything I'm missing. *Plié, attitude. That's it. Just get back in the groove.*

Straightening my leg out behind my body, I go into an *arabesque*. I place my left leg first on my right knee, then out behind me in a *pirouette*.

"Nice," says a voice from the doorway.

I spin around to see a girl watching me. She has the same curly blonde hair as Ms Jenkins. Her tap shoes *click-clack* with each step as she walks towards me.

"I'm Grace," she says with a smile.

Butterflies storm my stomach. "I'm Jada. I'm new?" It comes out like a question.

Grace looks me over, probably wondering how I measure up to the other dancers. I cross my arms protectively over my chest.

"How old are you?" she asks.

"Twelve," I say.

"That's my age group," Grace says.

She looks at me expectantly, but I'm not sure what I'm supposed to say. After a moment, Grace frowns. This is not going well.

"Do you mind if I warm up in here too?" Grace finally asks.

I shrug. *Why am I being so awkward?* I think. *Get it together, Jada.*

I try to go back to dancing, but my head isn't on warming up anymore. I have too many questions. Maybe they can help break the ice that's forming.

"So how do auditions work?" I ask, raising my voice to be heard above Grace's tapping.

Grace pauses to catch her breath. "Ms Marianne takes everyone one at a time, which lasts *forever*," she says. "It's easier to focus that way, though."

A private audition is a relief. At least then I won't have all the other girls watching – and judging – me. "How many girls usually get on to the team?"

Grace shrugs. "Depends on what's needed," she says. "At the competitions, awards are given in each age group, for each dance type. Ms Marianne always wants more girls for the ballet performance, so you probably have a good chance."

What's that supposed to mean? I think. *That I wouldn't have had a good chance otherwise?* It bothers me that I can't tell for certain what Grace is thinking. Back home, I knew exactly what my friends meant.

"We have to audition every year, even if we were on the team before," Grace continues, tapping her toes. "Past members audition with last year's routine. I was new last year, so I didn't know the routine for my first audition either. Ms Marianne told me to just practise some key moves for my audition."

Again, she stares at me expectantly, and again I stare back like a mannequin, not sure what to say.

Grace sighs and turns away to keep warming up.

"I've been practising my key ballet moves," I finally offer. But I'm not sure Grace hears me.

"Two minutes!" Ms Jenkins calls from the doorway. She scans the clipboard in her hand and smiles warmly. At least someone likes me.

"Jada," she says. "You're first."

CHAPTER 3

AUDITION TIME

Ms Jenkins leads me to the audition room. The dancers I spy along the way range in age. I can't help but wonder how I measure up.

Are my jumps as high? I think. *Are my turns as good?*

"Here we are," Ms Jenkins says, entering an empty studio. A floor-to-ceiling window takes up one whole wall.

"Wow," I whisper, forgetting my nerves.

Ms Jenkins smiles. "This is my favourite room."

"And mine." A tall woman in a leotard enters the room. She wears her hair in a sleek bun.

"Jada, this is Ms Marianne," says Ms Jenkins. "You're in good hands." She winks before leaving.

"It's so nice to meet you," Ms Marianne says.

"Same here." My voice squeaks.

"Your mother mentioned you've been dancing for almost seven years. Is that correct?"

I nod nervously.

"I know you aren't familiar with our routine from last year, but with that kind of experience, you'll be fine," Ms Marianne says. "Do you want to show me some of your key moves?"

My mouth is dry. "OK," I manage to say.

Ms Marianne starts to play a piano medley, and it's time to begin. I *plié to* start, then move into my combinations.

I raise my arms overhead into fifth position, arms curved and fingertips almost touching. Then I sweep my right toe across the floor and jump before doing the same thing with my left.

The piano notes quicken, and I *chassé* across the floor, my feet coming together with each jump. The music slows, and I do a *plié*, arms overhead.

Next I point my right toe. Using all my strength, I push off with my left leg, leaping into the air in a *jeté*. I can't help grinning as I land. That was the best one I've ever done. I could feel the power in my legs as I flew through the air.

As the music ends, I move my feet into first position. Heels touching, I sink into a final *plié*.

"Bravo!" Ms Marianne applauds.

"When will I find out if I've made the team?" I blurt out before I can stop myself.

"I'll post results tomorrow. You're welcome to bring a sleeping bag and hang around until then," she jokes.

I smile but think, *Little does she know I would jump at the chance to do that.*

CHAPTER 4

A NEW TEAM

When Mum drops me off the next day, I rush inside. There's already a crowd outside the office.

Ms Marianne, holding a piece of paper, walks into the middle of the crowd. "OK, girls, if your name is on this list, you've made the team. Practices will be from four to six, every Monday, Thursday and Saturday. Everyone must also take the Wednesday ballet class; it's the foundation of all dance disciplines."

My old dance school was the same way about ballet. That's how I became good friends with Maya and Natalie, even though we all focus on different dance styles.

"The first competition is in three weeks," Ms Marianne continues. "It's important, so please take it seriously. The first competition helps set the tone for the rest of the season. It will determine how you and your teammates dance together from here on out. It's an opportunity to be a part of something great."

My heart beats with excitement. This is what I've been missing – the chance to be a part of a team again. The chance to have good friends.

Ms Marianne tapes the list to the wall. Girls immediately start pushing forward, trying to read the names.

"I'm going to get trampled before I find out if I've made the team," I mutter.

Someone laughs. I turn and see Grace behind me. "Can't dance with broken legs," she agrees.

I smile. Today's chat seems to be going better than yesterday's.

"What's so funny?" another girl asks, walking over to join us. She's wearing jazz shoes and has her brown hair tied back with a ribbon.

"Hey, Gabby," Grace says. "Jada and I were just laughing about the chaos."

"Jada," says Gabby. She and Grace exchange a glance. An uneasy feeling builds up inside me.

A girl runs towards us. "Did we make the team?" she asks breathlessly. Her red cheeks match her backwards baseball cap, vest-top and trainers.

"Not sure yet," says Gabby. "Brie, this is Jada, the one Grace told us about."

Brie smiles shyly. "Hi."

"Hi," I say back.

"Assuming we've made the team, we're going to have our work cut out for us with the competition in three weeks," Grace says.

"It sounds like a big deal," I add.

Grace nods. "A *huge* deal. Because it's the first one, practising is that much more important. The new girls need to learn the steps in their dance."

That's exactly what I've been wanting – to practise with a team – so why are my palms immediately so sweaty?

"Even though we're stressed," chimes in Gabby, "it's a–"

"Good kind of stress," finishes Brie. She smiles at her friends, and the three of them link arms as they move closer to the front of the line.

"Jada," says Grace, motioning me over.

I can't tell if Grace really wants me to join or if she's just being nice. I decide to play it safe. "It's OK. I'm fine."

Frowning, Grace turns away. A moment later, she reaches the wall. "Finally!" I hear her exclaim.

I close my eyes. *Please let me get in. Please let me get in.*

"Yes!" I hear Brie and Gabby shout.

I open my eyes and take a step forward. My index finger shakes as I run it down the list of names – *Jada Grant.* I've made it!

I turn around, excited to tell the other girls. Gabby, Grace and Brie are all jumping up and down, their arms around each other. They don't even notice me.

I blink back tears and wonder how it's possible to feel so left out in the middle of a crowd.

CHAPTER 5

FiRST pRACTiCE

"And *plié*," Ms Marianne says to our ballet group two days later.

All ten dancers hold onto the barre and bend our knees. This first practice reminds me of practices back at home – a sea of girls in buns, leotards and ballet slippers, all moving together.

"Please begin your warm-ups," Ms Marianne instructs.

I shift my left heel to the centre of my right foot. Then I raise my left arm high overhead, keeping my right arm to the side.

I swallow a lump in my throat as I realize everyone else is doing warm-ups with a partner. I remember how Natalie, Maya and I used to do the same.

I move my arms high above my head, and my feet move into fifth position, the left toe touching the right heel.

Once everyone has finished warming up, Ms Marianne gathers us together. "This routine will have a combination of *pirouettes* and *grand jetés*," she explains. "Watch me." She *chassés* across the floor before flying through the air, legs split.

One grand jeté, I count. *Two, three.*

Ms Marianne barely pauses to touch the ground. After the final *grand jeté*, she turns across the floor, her body spinning quickly with each *pirouette*.

One, two, three, I count again.

"Make sure you spot. We can't have dizzy ballerinas," Ms Marianne reminds us as she finishes.

Everyone breaks apart to practise the routine. I fly through the jumps, but the *pirouettes* are harder. I only manage to do one perfectly. The second is much harder, and by the time I get to the third, I lose focus and stumble.

Focus, I tell myself. *If you can't keep up at practice, how do you expect to be ready for the competition? It's going to set the tone for the whole season.*

I glance around the room. I'm not the only one struggling, but somehow that doesn't make me feel any better.

CHAPTER 6

DANCER DOWN

For two days, I do nothing but practise my foot positions, *grand jetés* and *pirouettes*. By the time Wednesday's first all-team ballet class comes around, I'm getting better with spotting. But I still can't do three *pirouettes* in a row without getting dizzy.

Practice starts in half an hour, so I decide to take advantage of the quiet and try again. But before I can, my phone buzzes with a text from Maya:

We're practising today! Miss you!

Then one from Natalie:

Doing my jumps and thinking of you!

I smile. It's almost like my old dance team and I are practising together.

Putting my phone down, I *chassé* down the hardwood floor and leap into the air. My feet brush the floor and fly up again. I repeat the move for my third *grand jeté*.

"Nice height," someone says.

I turn and see Grace, Gabby and Brie standing near the doorway. "Thanks. Were you all there long?" I ask.

Grace shrugs. "Long enough."

Brie clears her throat. "You're good," she says quietly.

They're being nice, I think. *Just act normal.* "Thank you," I say.

The three of them move to the barre to begin their warm-ups. Gabby makes a comment I can't hear, and Brie and Grace giggle at whatever she said.

I remember the inside jokes Maya, Natalie and I shared during warm-ups. Would it have been weird if someone new tried to join in? I don't want them to think I'm trying to wedge myself into their group.

Not wanting to risk it, I walk to the far end of the studio to practise my *grand jetés* and *pirouettes*. My body soars for the jumps, but the *pirouettes* are another story. I slump to the floor and smack the wood with my hand in frustration.

"Hey," Brie calls gently.

I raise my head, feeling silly for showing my feelings.

"Sharing hard moves helps me," Brie says. "Do you want to show us?"

Fresh eyes usually help me too, but I still feel self-conscious around them. *You're on the same team*, I remind myself. "I suppose?"

Gabby rolls her eyes, and Grace shoots her a look. Then she turns to me and sucks in her cheeks, pretending to be Ms Marianne. "And a one, and a two."

I smile nervously. I raise my left foot to my right knee and turn, arms curved in front of me. I swivel my head quickly, focusing on one spot to keep my balance, just like I've been practising.

So far so good. I spin again, but this time I stumble.

"Grrr!" I say. "See?"

Gabby nods. "Maybe you just need a mental break. It looked like you didn't spot the last one."

I bristle. *I tried to spot it.*

"I picked that small crack in the wall to spot," I tell her. "My eyes found it the first time, but then . . . I'll try one more time."

"Are you sure?" Grace asks. "You don't want to tire yourself out before practice."

"I'll be fine," I snap.

The first competition is less than three weeks away. As Grace said before, it's a big deal. I have to get this right. There's no other choice. I don't need the other dancers thinking the new girl can't take it.

I focus on the squiggly crack in the wall as I spin my body around. *One, two . . .*

My eyes find the spot easily, and my left leg moves behind me as I turn.

I can do this, I think. *Just one more.*

I find the spot again, and my body moves for the last spin. Suddenly I'm losing balance, and I can't get it back. My leg slips from my knee, and I feel myself falling.

In an instant, I'm on the floor. Pain shoots through my ankle, and I scream.

Feet rush towards me. "Can you stand?" someone asks.

The pain is so bad, I can't tell who's speaking. My ankle throbs, and the room spins.

"Jada, are you OK?" someone else asks. I think it's Grace.

Bile rises to my throat. There are so many voices, so many feet running around. My ankle is killing me and so is my pride. Seconds ago, I was worried about completing the perfect *pirouette*. Now I can't even stand.

"Jada!" someone else calls.

I just want everyone to go away. Why did this have to happen? I close my eyes.

"Leave me alone!" I shout.

Then there's only quiet.

CHAPTER 7

WHAT NOW?

Two hours later, Dad and I are at the doctor's awaiting the verdict. Dad sits beside me. "I bet it's minor," he says in his confident voice.

"Doesn't feel minor," I mutter.

Dad squeezes my hand. "Try to be positive."

I glare at him. I have no friends here, and any chance of being a part of the team is gone. There's no reason to be positive.

Before I can reply, Dr Hutchinson walks in. "You're lucky," he says. "It's just a minor sprain, and–"

"Why does it hurt so much?" I interrupt.

"Ankles are funny things," Dr Hutchinson says, shrugging.

I glare at him. There is *nothing* funny about this.

Dr Hutchinson stays upbeat. "Ice it every half an hour, and stay off it for the rest of the day. If the swelling goes down tomorrow, some pressure is fine." He hands me a leaflet of instructions. "Start these stretching exercises in two days. Sprains usually heal in a week, ten days max."

"I have a dance competition in two-and-a-half weeks," I say nervously.

"You should be fine," he says optimistically.

What if he's wrong? I worry. *What if I miss the first competition? I'll never get that back. I'll never be a part of the team.*

"And if I'm not?" I ask shakily. "Then what happens?"

"If there's a problem," says Dr Hutchinson, "we'll deal with it in ten days."

* * *

When I get home, I text Maya: *I hurt my ankle. :-(*

She texts back immediately: *Is it bad? :(*

Doc says will heal in 10 days.

In time for your first competition!

So he claims.

Bet your dad told you to stay positive. ;-)

LOL you know my fam well.

The conversation makes me smile, but it also makes me sad. I miss home. I miss not feeling like I have to prove something. I miss having friends.

I turn off my phone and close my eyes. Maybe when I wake up, I'll realize this has all been a bad dream.

CHAPTER 8

ANKLE ANGST

When I wake up the next day and turn my phone back on, it's filled with texts. I hope it's my new teammates. They could have got my number if they'd wanted. I deflate when I see none of the texts are from them.

Maya told me about your ankle! You OK? writes Natalie.

We're thinking about you! Maya texts.

I reply to the group text:

In paaain. Wish you both were here!

"How did you sleep?" Mum asks, walking into my room with an ice pack in hand.

I shrug.

She leans down to look at my ankle. "Looks like the swelling is down!"

"Still hurts," I mutter.

Mum places the ice pack on my ankle. "We'll keep icing. Maybe you'll be able to put weight on it by the end of the day."

"Doubt it," I grumble.

"Ms Marianne called," Mum continues cheerfully. "She's hoping you can come to practice tomorrow."

"What for?" I snap. "No one there likes me anyway."

Mum sits down. "Why do you think that?"

"Because it's obvious. I can tell! I wish you'd never made me move to this stupid town. I hate it here!" I throw a pillow across the room.

Mum gives me a stern look. "I know you're in pain, but you don't get to speak to me like that. I'm here if you want to *talk,* not *yell.*"

She leaves the room, and I cross my arms and flop my head back on the bed. The sudden movement makes my ankle throb.

"Fine!" I yell. I wait for my mum to yell something back, but the only reply is silence.

* * *

The next morning, I limp into the kitchen. Mum is already there. Before I can say anything, she says, "I called Dr Hutchinson. He said walking on your ankle and doing the stretching exercises will make it heal faster."

"But the swelling–" I start.

"Is down," she finishes.

Her tone makes it clear arguing isn't going to get me anywhere. Irritated, I turn to go back upstairs and stumble, putting all my weight on my ankle. "Ow!"

"Do you want to lean on me?" Mum asks.

"No!" I snap. "I don't need your help. If you hadn't made me move here and join this stupid team, none of this would have happened." Tears are streaming down my cheeks now.

My mum tries to put her arm around me, but I push it away. "I'm fine! You wanted me to go to practice, and I'm going!" I hobble up the stairs and slam my bedroom door.

I know I'm being a brat, but I can't seem to stop myself. I feel so alone. None of my teammates even care that I'm injured. And if I'm not there for the first competition, I might as well give up. I'll never be a part of the team. Screaming is easier than dealing with all of that.

CHAPTER 9

FACING THE MUSIC

"Jada!" says Ms Marianne when my mum and I sit down just outside the ballet studio. "I'm so glad you came!" She gives me a hug.

I'm embarrassed I was so against coming. "Thanks for inviting me," I say.

"How's your ankle?" she asks.

I shrug. "Still hurts, but I'm hoping it will heal by the first competition. I know it's a big deal–"

Ms Marianne puts her hand on my shoulder. "It's just one day."

"But–" I interrupt.

"It's *one* day, Jada," she says again. "You'll be on the team with these girls for the whole *year*. Just focus on getting better." She walks into the studio.

I slump down in my seat. No one understands.

Inside the studio, the music begins. I watch through the window as the girls start with *pliés*, moving their feet to first and second position. Their arms curve in front of them and then move overhead. Their feet *chassé* down the dance floor.

The *attitude* and *arabesque* are next. I so want to be out there. My body tenses as the dancers ready themselves for the *grand jetés*.

One, two, three. They land perfectly and turn their bodies for the *pirouettes*. Their feet barely touch their knees before quickly moving behind them for the turns.

Ms Marianne has added an *assemblé*, one of my favourite jumps. The girls begin in fifth position, the toes of each foot touching the opposite heels. They jump, feet meeting in mid-air, then land in fifth again.

I close my eyes and pretend I'm dancing with them.

"Hello," says Grace's voice behind me.

I open my eyes, realizing practice has ended, and turn around.

I swallow. "Hi."

Grace shifts from one foot to the other. "How are you?"

I shrug. "Not great."

"We've missed you," she says.

"I doubt that," I mutter.

Grace looks surprised. "What do you mean?"

My mum clears her throat. I'd almost forgotten she was there.

"I'm going to check on something in the office," she says. She squeezes my shoulder before she goes.

"It's just . . .," I begin. "It didn't seem like you guys really liked me." My voice is small.

Grace sits beside me. "Seriously? Every time we tried talking to you, you hardly said anything. When we stretched for the ballet class, you stayed away from us. Even when we wanted to help with your ballet routine, you seemed annoyed. We thought *you* didn't like *us*."

I look down at my hands. I don't know what to say. As I replay the scenes in my mind, I realize maybe they *were* making an effort. Maybe I was the one pushing them away.

"I didn't mean to yell at you when I hurt my ankle. I was just so scared and embarrassed," I say, still looking at my hands.

"I would have been scared too," Grace says.

I slowly raise my head. Grace is smiling. I smile back and extend my hand. "Can we start again? I'm Jada, and I'm new."

Grace laughs. "I've seen you dance. You're good. I'm Grace."

Just then Brie and Gabby walk up. Grace puts her arm around me. "I'd like you both to meet Jada, a new friend of mine."

Gabby and Brie exchange confused looks, then seem to understand. "Hi, Jada," says Gabby. "Welcome to the team."

Brie smiles, a bit shy. "You'll like it here," she says.

I smile, and Grace says, "OK, so tell us – what's going on with your ankle?"

"It's a minor sprain," I say. "The doctor said stretching and walking on it will help."

"Has it helped?" asks Brie.

"I haven't really tried," I admit.

"We'll help," says Gabby. "If you want us to."

I look at the other girls. The competition is only two weeks away, but maybe that doesn't matter. I can be a part of a team again, if I change my attitude and face my fears.

I swallow. "I'd like your help," I say quietly.

Grace extends her arm, and I lean on it. "Are you OK?" she asks.

I nod. "I can take it from here." I put more weight on my ankle. It hurts, but not as much as I thought it would. I walk a few steps, then sit back down.

"Was that awful?" asks Grace.

"It wasn't fun, but the pain I built up in my head was worse than the real thing," I say.

"First competition, here you come!" says Gabby.

"If you need to chat or anything, we're here," says Brie. "Have you got your phone?"

I nod and hand it over. Brie, Grace and Gabby enter their phone numbers. I enter mine into their phones too. By the time my mum comes back, the four of us are laughing.

"Looks like I've missed something," Mum says.

"I'll fill you in during our stretching exercises." I smile at her.

She raises an eyebrow. "That sounds like a good plan."

Gabby, Grace and Brie give me a hug before my mum and I go outside. I limp to the car.

"Are you OK?" asks my mum.

My phone buzzes with a group text from Gabby, Brie and Grace. *You can do this!*

I smile. "Yes," I say. "I'm definitely OK."

CHAPTER 10

BACK AT THE BARRE

The following Saturday, ten days after I hurt my ankle, I'm back at the doctor's. The competition is only a week away. I've been doing my stretches – both at home and at the dance studio. My new teammates have been a huge help in keeping me on track. But even if I don't make it to the competition, I know I'm still a part of the team.

I hold my breath as Dr Hutchinson wraps his fingers around my ankle. When he presses, I wince reflexively.

He frowns. "Did that hurt?"

"No," I admit. "I just thought it would."

Dr Hutchinson laughs. "Don't scare me like that." He flexes and points my foot. Still no pain.

"I'm afraid . . .," he begins, as I hold my breath, "we won't be seeing each other anymore."

I hop down from the table, landing on my ankle. "It's like nothing ever happened!"

"It pays to be positive," Dad says.

He's right. When I finally gave my new friends a chance and focused on recovery, everything fell into place.

"Yeah, yeah," I say, grinning.

Dad's eyes twinkle. "Maybe hurting your ankle was a blessing."

I laugh. "I wouldn't go that far!"

* * *

"Small jumps," Ms Marianne says at Monday's ballet practice. "Four *sautés*."

We place our feet in first position, heels touching, and lower ourselves into a *plié*. Then we jump up, legs together, and lower ourselves into a *plié* position again.

"And one, and two, and three, and four," Ms Marianne counts.

When the warm-up is finished, Ms Marianne puts on our competition song. I recognize it from all the time I've spent watching the other dancers practise this week.

Practising the dance in my mind has helped. All the ballerinas *chassé* across the floor in unison. We raise our legs for the *arabesques* and *attitudes* and leap for the *assemblés*.

Here we go, I think as the final sequence nears.

We rise high in the air, legs in split position, for the *grand jetés*. For the last *grand jeté*, we jump, one row after the other.

The *pirouettes* are last. We place our legs on our knees and turn. I pick the corner of the wall to spot. *One. Two.* My eyes find the corner quickly. *And three.* I hold my breath and turn, my head quickly swivelling to find the corner again. *You can do this.*

As the music finishes, we face Ms Marianne. I didn't stumble at all.

Ms Marianne claps her hands. "Beautiful!"

I breathe a sigh of relief. The competition is less than a week away, and my ankle and I are both ready.

CHAPTER 11

THE COMPETITION

I stand backstage at the competition venue, watching the other teams perform. My hair is tucked tightly into a bun, and glittery eyeshadow and lipstick glimmer on my face.

"This is it," Gabby whispers.

The ballet group and I practised every day this week, and I didn't fumble once. I know I can do the spins and jumps ahead of me, but my stomach is in knots anyway.

"You'll be great," says Brie.

Ms Marianne motions for the ballerinas to get ready.

Grace squeezes my hand. "You can do this, teammate," she says.

The rest of the ballerinas and I move into position, and I smooth my hands over my white, sequined leotard. Then the curtain goes up, the music begins, and my feet move as if on their own.

My knees bend as I *plié* and then effortlessly move to first and second positions. My arms curve in front of me and then above my head. I join the sea of ballerinas as we raise our legs in *attitude* and straighten them for *arabesque*.

Moving in sync, we place our feet in fifth position before completing the *assemblés*. Then we leap into the air, landing with soft thumps onto the floor.

The music speeds up for the *grand jetés*. I feel like a fairy fluttering through the air, legs in a split. I finish my last *grand jeté*.

Next I move quickly into a *pirouette*. My eyes find the edge of a curtain and follow it.

I turn. *One.* My foot quickly meets my knee again for the second spin. *Two.* Only one spin left. My foot glides behind me for the last *pirouette. Three.*

As the piano music slows, each girl moves her arms forward and finishes in first position. The audience applauds, and we bow before leaving the stage.

There are still several more ballet groups who will dance before scores can be posted, but scores aren't what's most important to me. Being able to dance with my team – my new team – matters most.

Brie, Grace and Gabby hurry over and sweep me into a group hug. Grace squeezes my shoulder and smiles.

"That was great!" she exclaims.

I smile back. I think about how I watched from the outside as Gabby, Brie and Grace huddled together when they found out they'd made the team. Now I'm part of their huddle. Being friends with these girls makes me feel like I belong.

As I look around at my dance team, I'm grateful I didn't let my fear ruin everything. I almost missed out on the good things about this town – like this group of girls. Nowhere is perfect. I know that now. But I also know, despite missing my old home, I'm going to like my new home.

ABOUT THE AUTHOR

Margaret Gurevich is the author of many books for children, including *Gina's Balance, Aerials and Envy* and the award-winning Chloe by Design series. She has also written for *National Geographic Kids* and Penguin Young Readers. While Margaret hasn't done performance dance since she was a tween, this series has inspired her to take dance classes again. She lives in New York, USA, with her son and husband.

ABOUT THE ILLUSTRATOR

Claire Almon lives and works in Georgia, USA, and holds a BFA in illustration from Ringling College of Art and Design, as well as an MFA in animation from Savannah College of Art and Design. She has worked for clients such as American Greetings, Netflix, and Cartoon Network and has taught character design at Savannah College of Art and Design. Claire specializes in creating fun, dynamic characters and works in a variety of mediums, including watercolours, pen and ink, pastel and digital.

GLOSSARY

competition contest between two or more rivals

deflate lose confidence or feel discouraged

discipline different area within the study of dance, such as ballet or jazz

fumble do something clumsily

routine part of an act or a performance that is carefully worked out so it can be repeated often

sprain sudden or severe twisting of a joint with stretching or tearing of ligaments

sulk be sullenly silent or irritable

unison two or more people performing the same movement at the same time

TALK ABOUT IT!

1. Talk about Jada's attitude after she injured her ankle. Do you think she was right to be upset? Why or why not?

2. Have you ever been the new person on a team or in a group? Talk about how that felt and what you did to ease any nerves you had.

3. Jada's mum tells her it's important for her to go to practice, even though she can't dance, because teammates support each other. Do you think this was fair? Talk about why you agree or disagree.

WRITE ABOUT IT!

1. Pretend you are Jada. Write a letter to your friends back home telling them about your new dance studio.

2. Write a chapter that continues this story. Who do you think wins the first dance competition?

3. Imagine you are Grace, Brie or Gabby. Write a few paragraphs describing meeting Jada for the first time.

BALLET GLOSSARY

arabesque position in ballet in which the body is bent forward from the hip on one leg with one arm extended forward and the other arm and leg backward

attitude ballet position, similar to the arabesque, in which the raised leg is bent at the knee

chassé gliding step in which one foot is kept in front of the other

grand jeté jump, or jeté, preceded by a high kick, in which a dancer leaps from one leg and lands on the other

jeté jump forwards, backwards or to the side, from one foot to the other

pirouette whirling about on one foot or on the points of the toes

plié movement in which the knees are bent while the back is held straight

BALLET POSITIONS

first position easiest, most basic foot position; stand with your heels together and toes facing equally out to either side

second position very similar to first position, except feet should be about hip distance apart; legs and feet should be equally turned out

third position start in first position, then move the heel of one foot to the middle of the other foot; legs should stay straight, with feet and legs equally turned out

fourth position place one foot in front of the other, about a foot's distance apart, with the heel of the front foot lined up with the toes of the back foot. Legs and feet should be equally turned out away from the centre of the body.

fifth position most difficult foot position; stand with your feet close together, one in front of the other and turned out away from your body

THE FUN DOESN'T STOP HERE!

DISCOVER MORE AT
WWW.RAINTREE.CO.UK